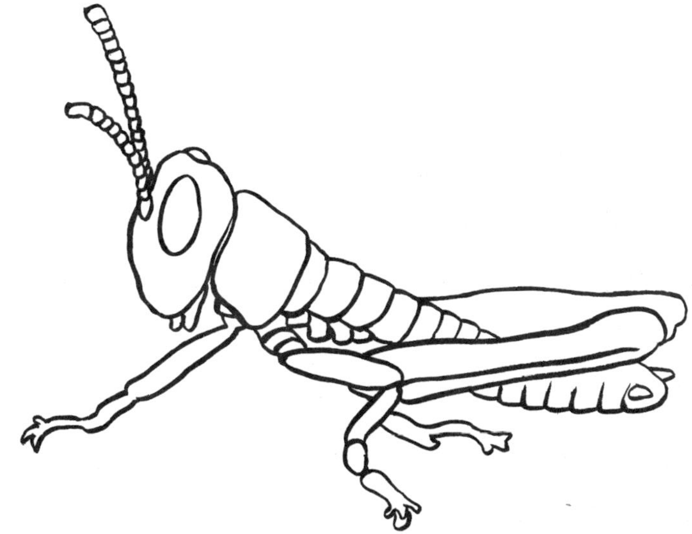

Australian Insects Colour and Learn

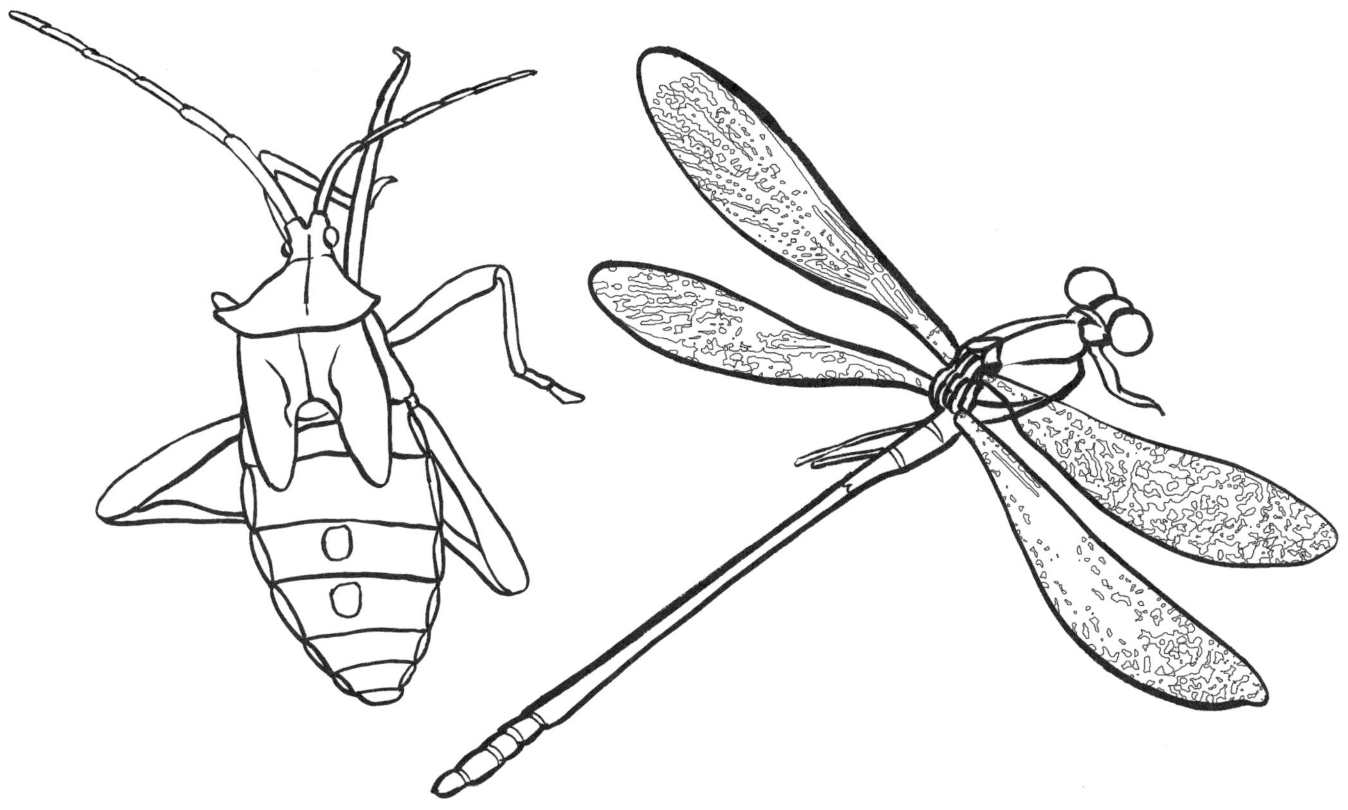

Although they do not sting or bite, many hoverflies have yellow and black striped patterns on their bodies, which resemble those of bees and wasps – this helps to deter predators from trying to eat them. Hoverflies are pollinators of many plants, including important crops.

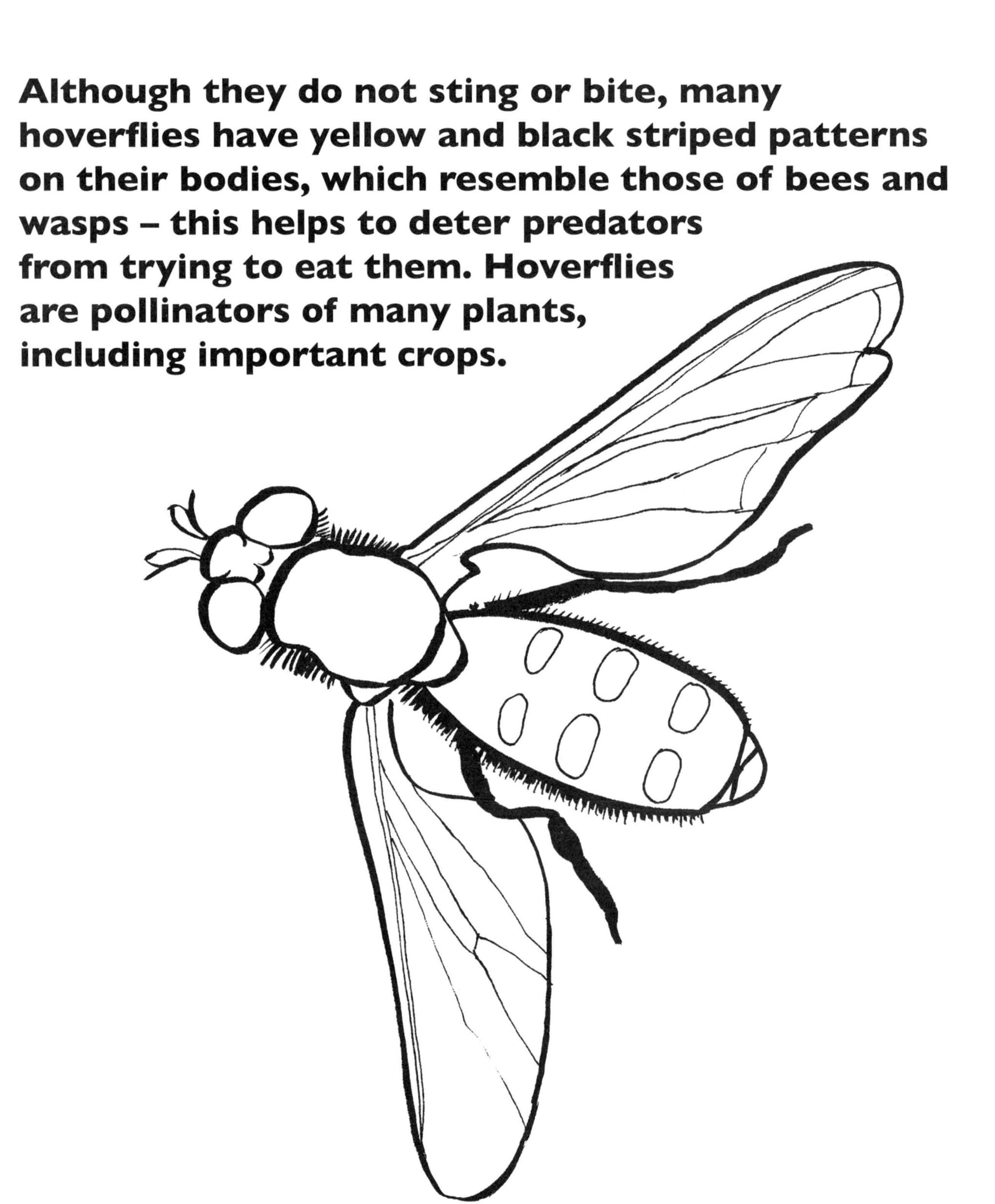

Hoverfly

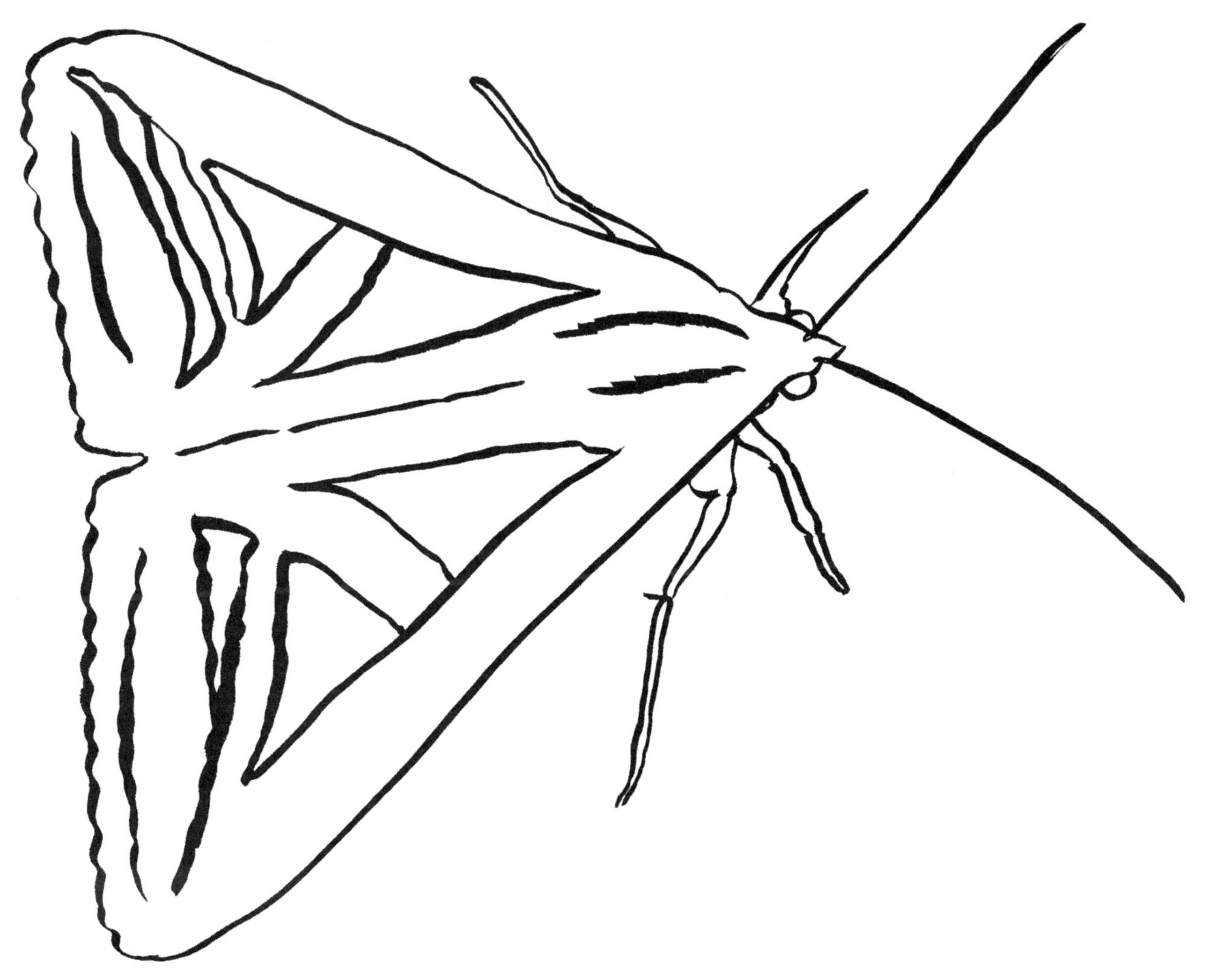

There are a large number of species in the geometrid moth family and many have amazing triangular patterns on their wings. Moths are in the same family as butterflies – known as Lepidoptera – and like butterflies their babies are caterpillars which feed on plants.

Geometrid Moth

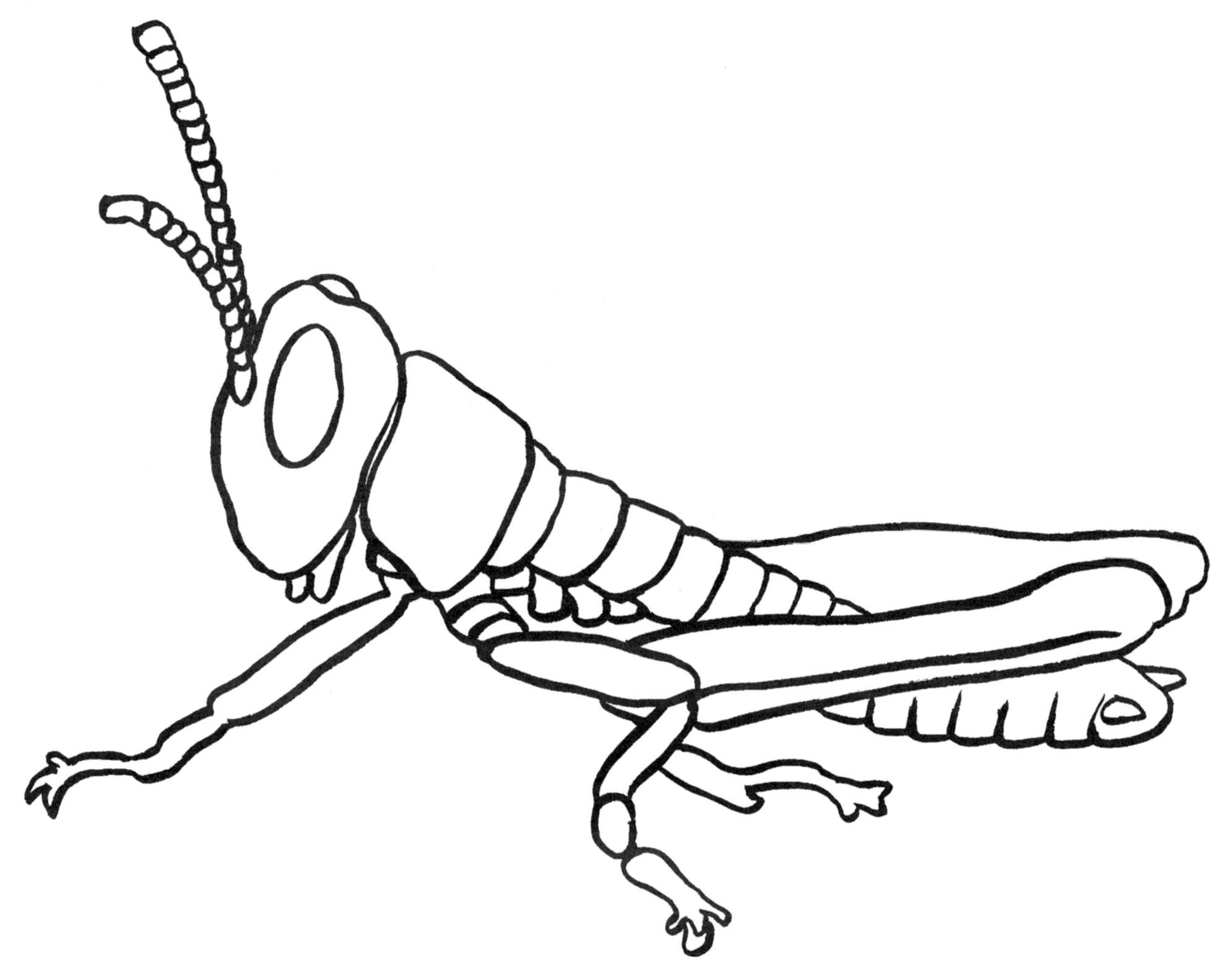

The amazing long hind legs enable these insects to jump incredible distances – sometimes more than 200 times their own length, which can mean leaps of several metres. The green and brown colours help them to blend in and hide amongst leaves and grasses.

Grasshopper

These bugs, which have a distinctive oval, shield-shaped body, are found all around Australia. They have mouthparts shaped like a drinking straw, which they use to pierce plants and drink the sap. If threatened they produce a smelly liquid to defend themselves.

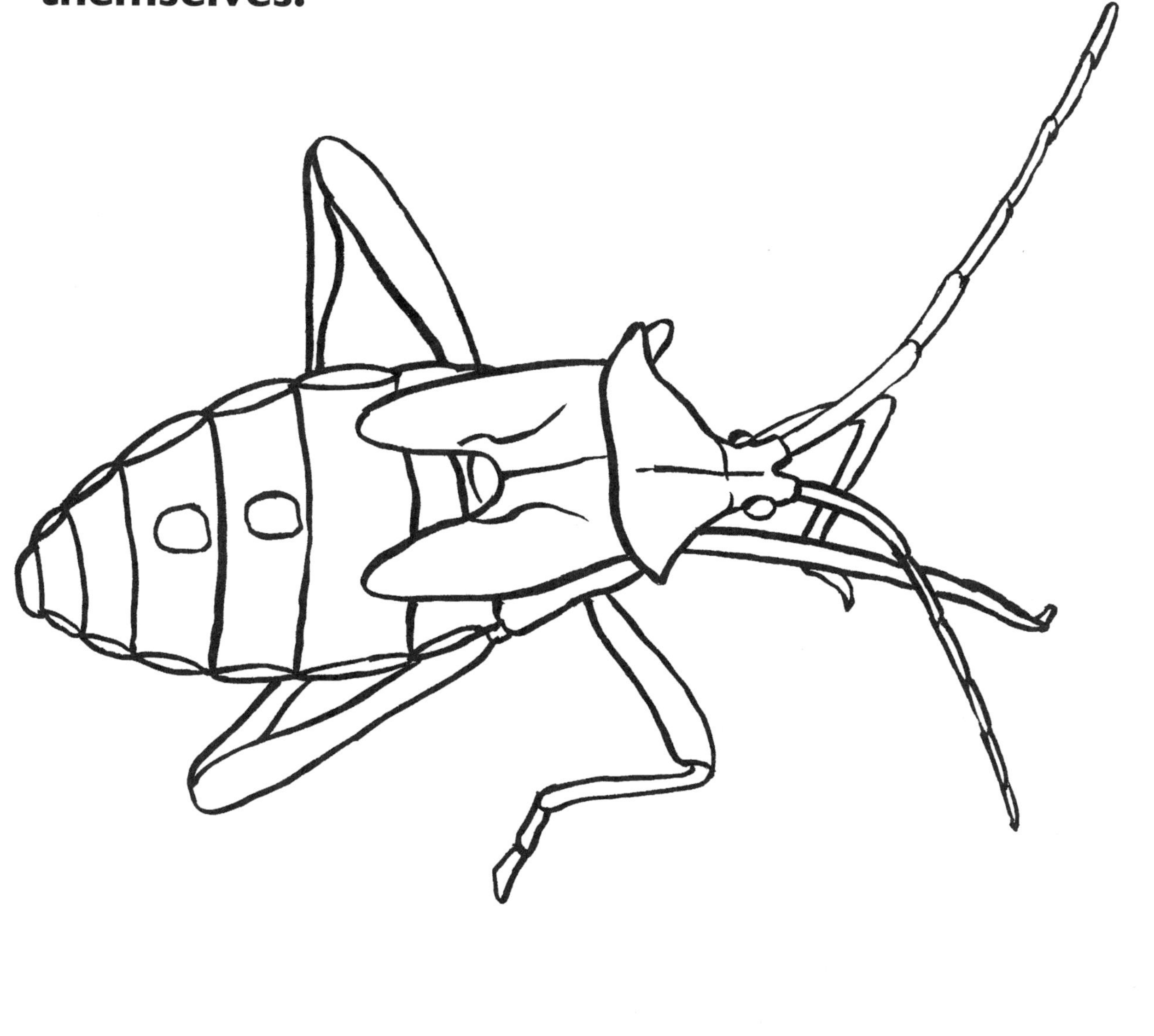

Crusader Bug

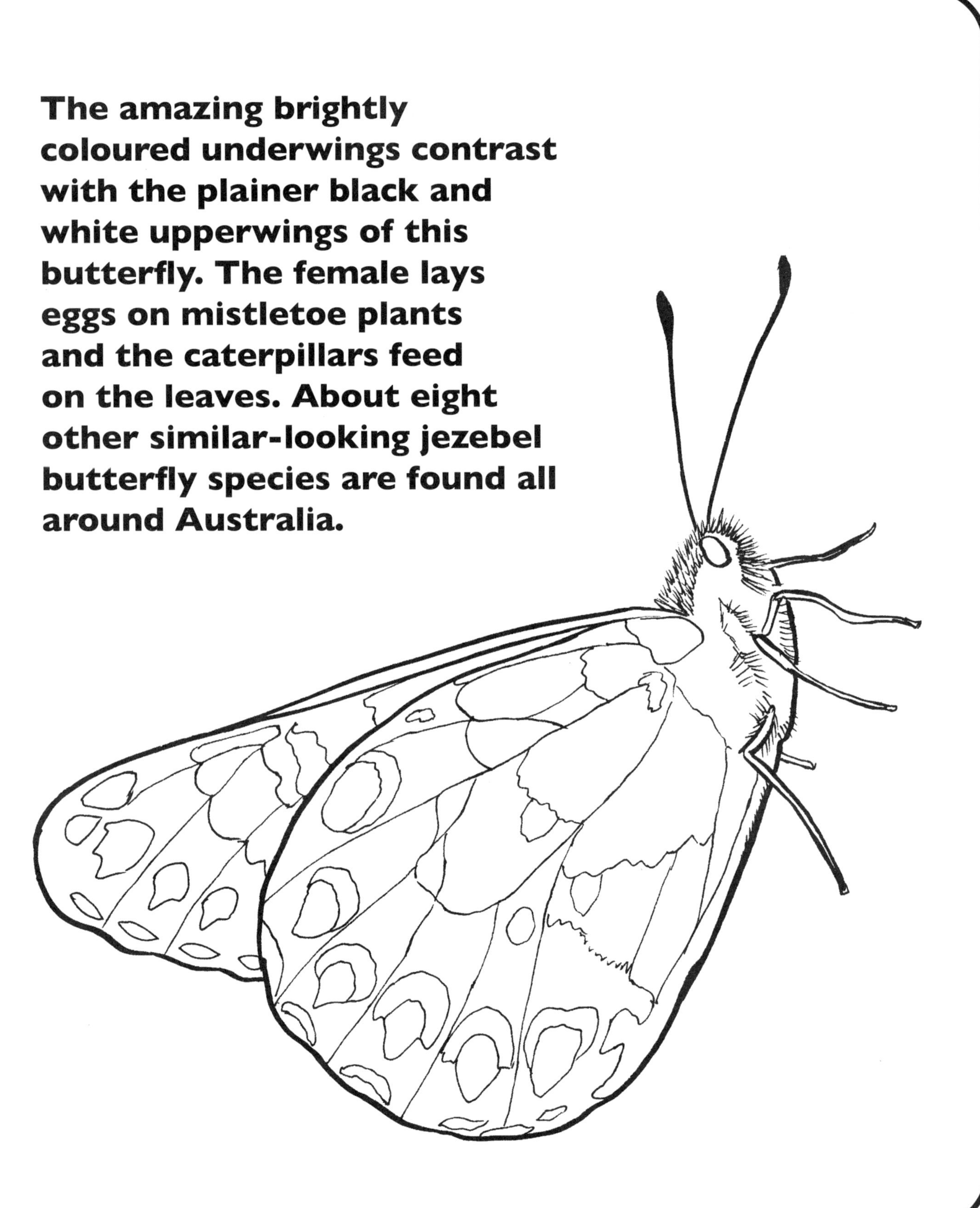

The amazing brightly coloured underwings contrast with the plainer black and white upperwings of this butterfly. The female lays eggs on mistletoe plants and the caterpillars feed on the leaves. About eight other similar-looking jezebel butterfly species are found all around Australia.

Spotted Jezebel Butterfly

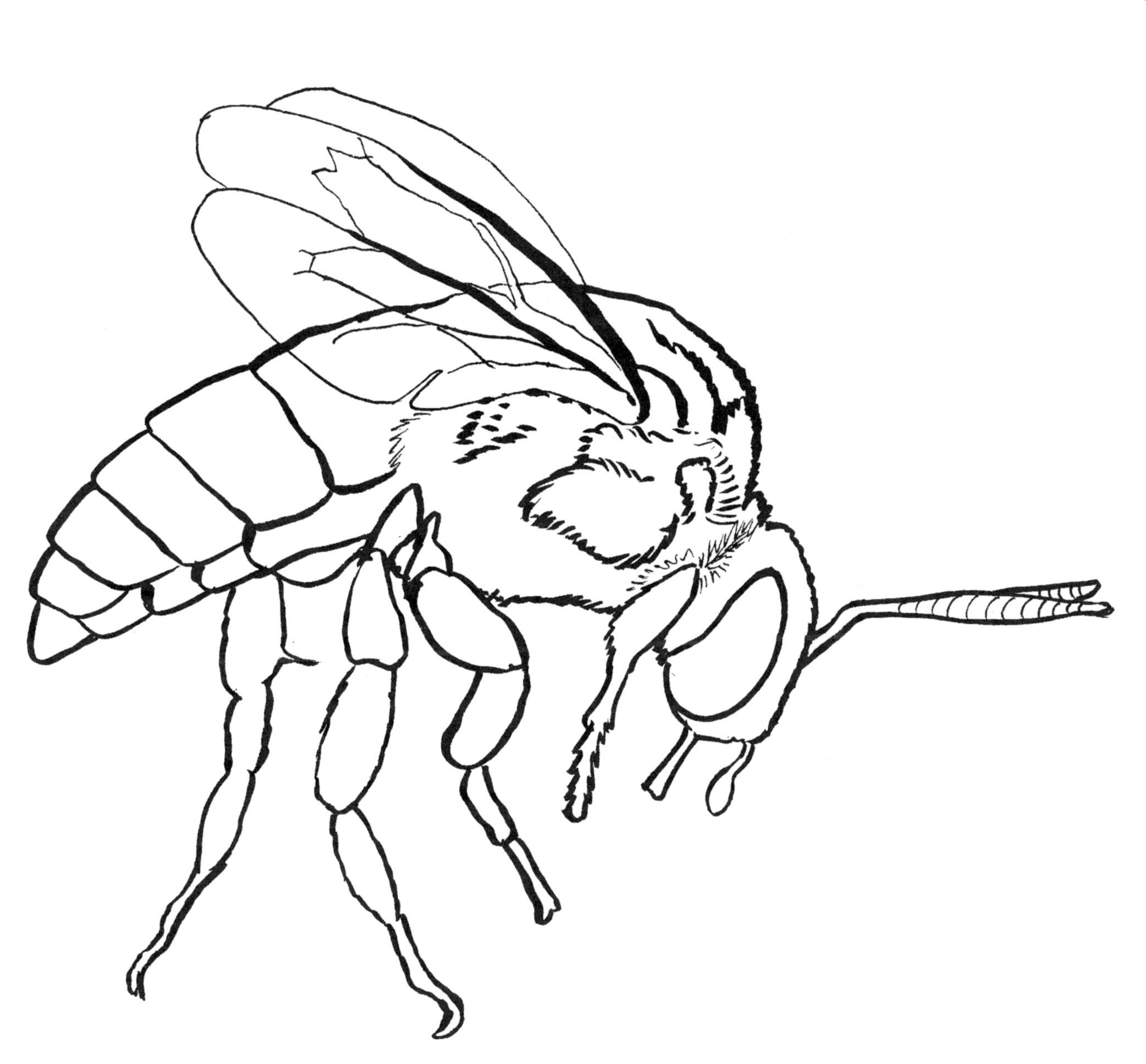

In this unusual bee species the yellow stripes are replaced by blue ones. Like their bird namesakes, cuckoo bees are parasites of other species' nests. The female lays eggs in other bees' nests and leaves them to be brought up by the hosts.

Neon Cuckoo Bee

These wonderful bugs are harmless and are popular as pets. Amazing camouflage helps them to exactly mimic the look of a dead leaf. If spotted by a potential predator they curl up their tail in a threat display that mimics a scorpion.

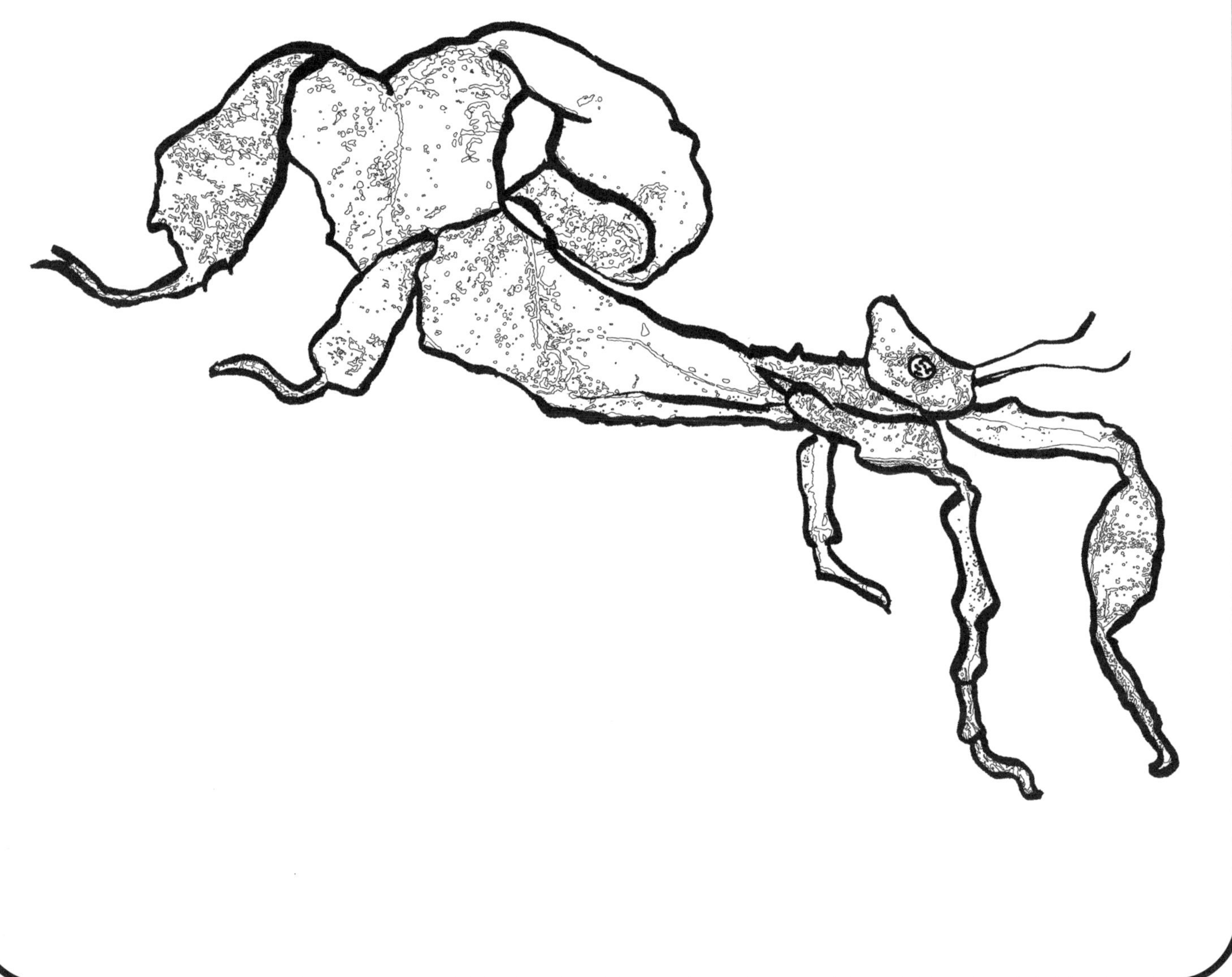

Spiny Leaf Insect

Growing up to 8cm in length, these insects dig burrows up to one metre underground in tropical rainforests. They are a vital part of the ecosystem because they help to recycle dead leaves from the forest floor. Like the leaf insect they are often kept as pets.

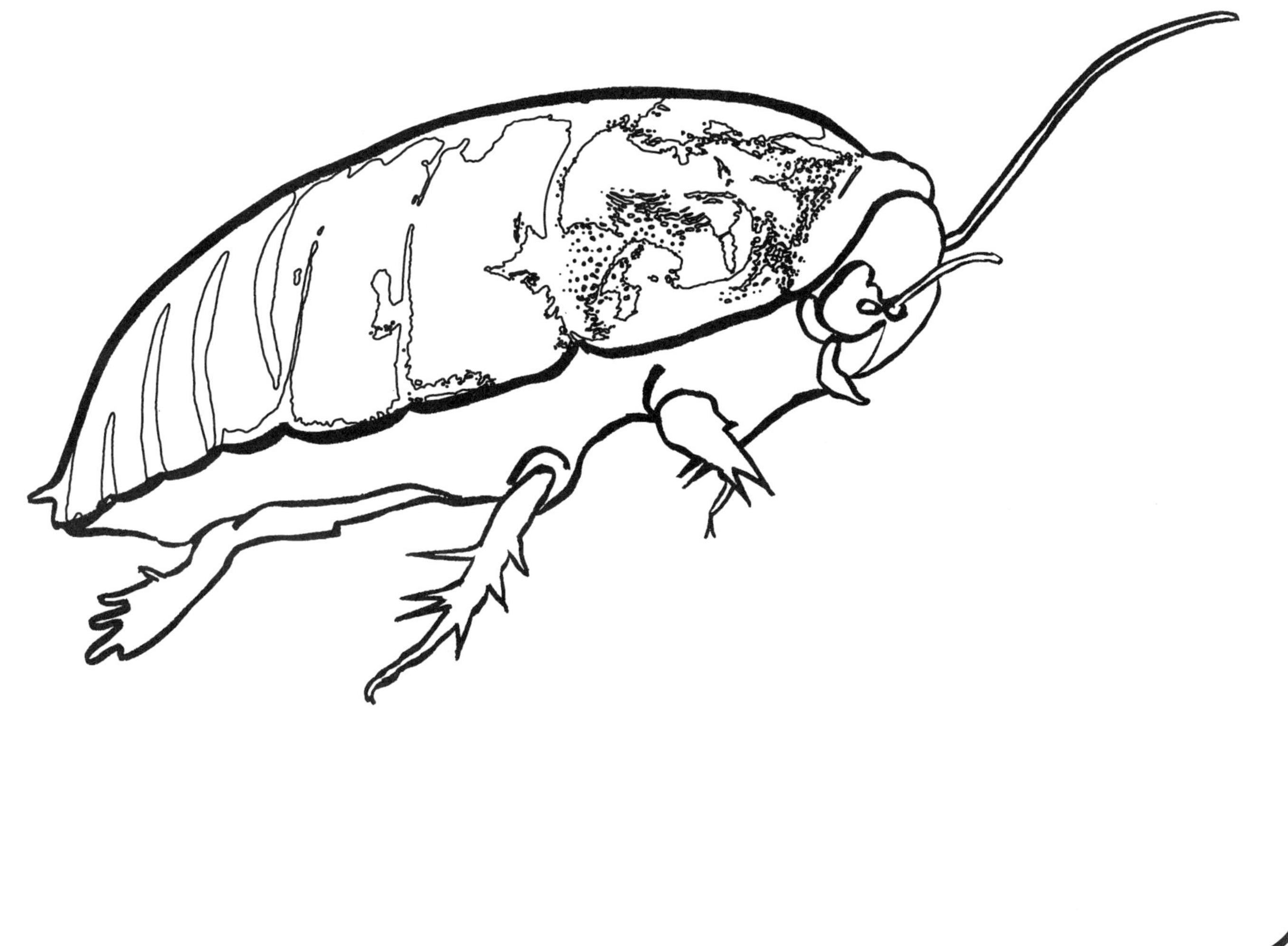

Giant Burrowing Cockroach

With wings the size of a dinner plate these are the biggest moths in Australia. The adults don't have mouthparts so they do not feed – their only job is to mate and lay eggs that will produce the next generation of the species.

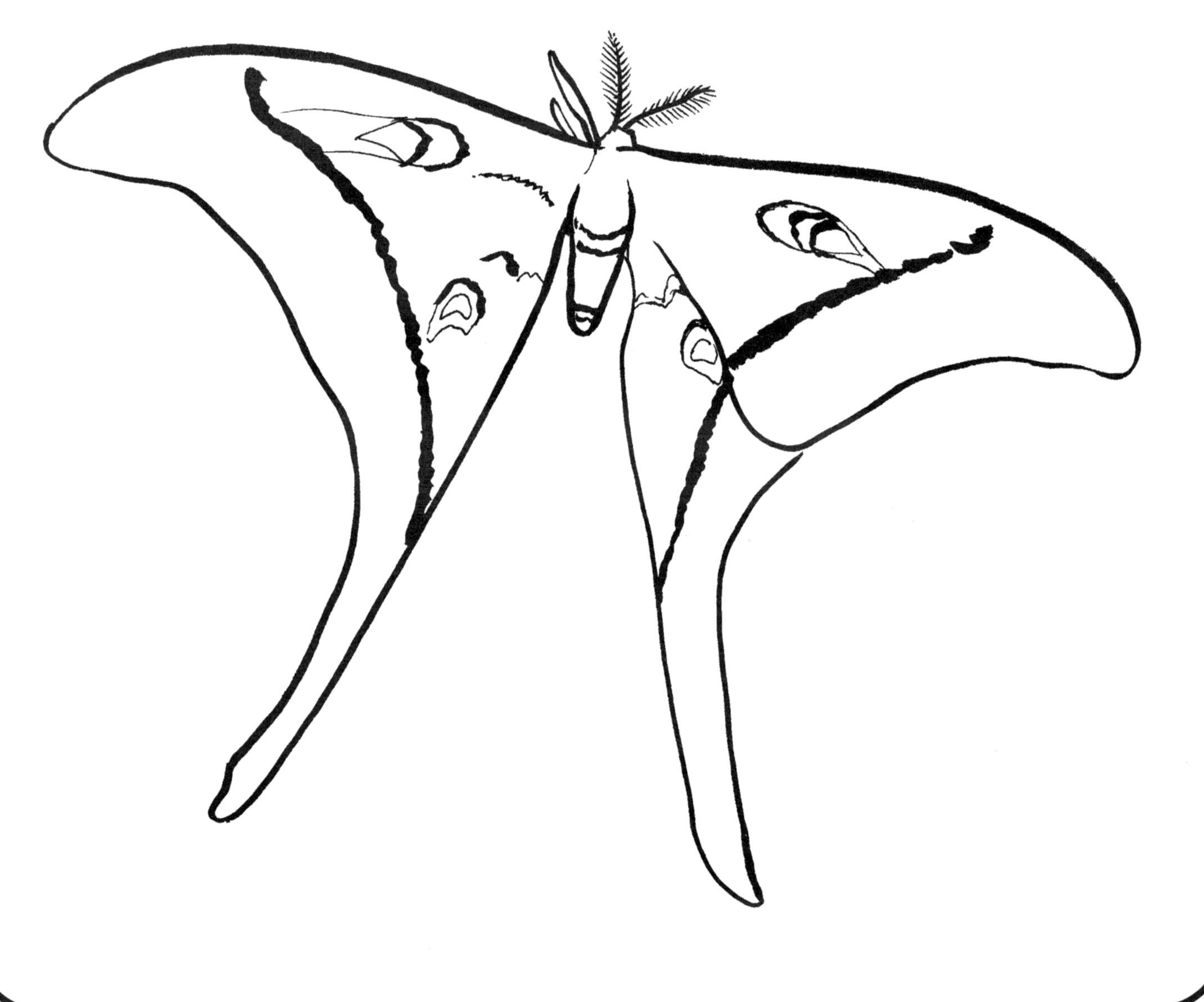

Hercules Moth

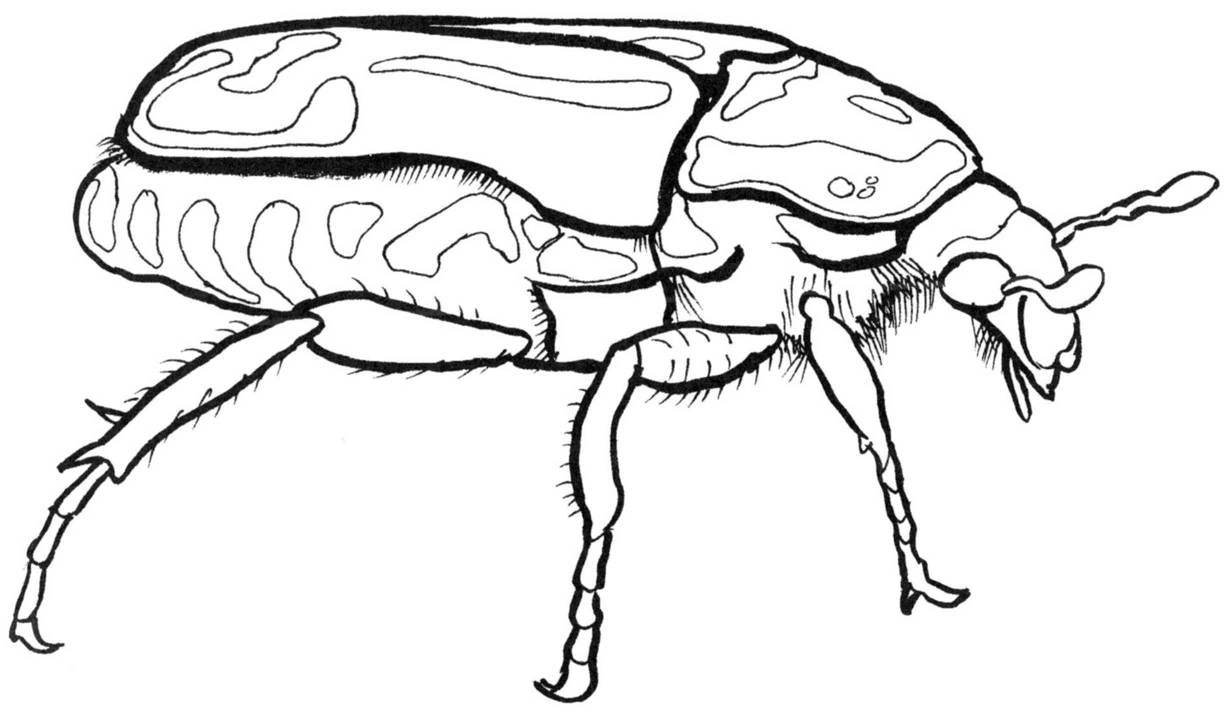

One of the most distinctive of the thousands of beetle species found in Australia. Named because the bright green markings form the shape of a violin on the beetle's back. The grubs live in rotting wood and the adults emerge to feed on nectar from flowers.

Fiddler Beetle

Harmless to humans, these amazing predators feed on other insects such as mosquitoes and can often be seen flying around wetlands. They lay their eggs under water and the young nymphs feed on aquatic insects and even small fish.

Dragonfly

It is easy to see why these beetles were given their name. The male's amazing rhino-like horn is used for fighting other males. There are many different species in Australia and although they look dangerous they are harmless to humans.

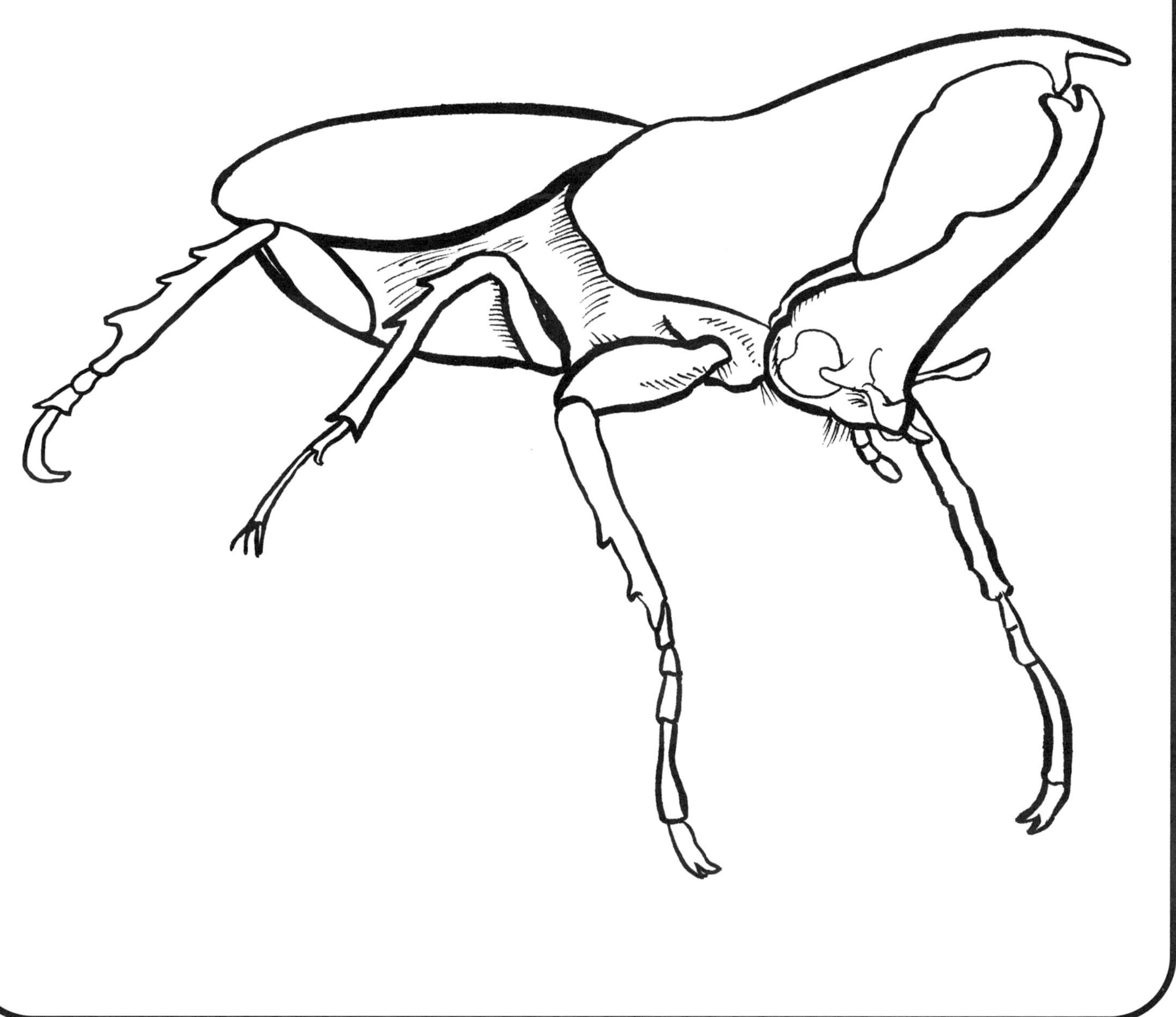

Rhinoceros Beetle

These distinctive large butterflies have a wingspan of 10cm and are common and widespread. The caterpillars feed on poisonous milkweed plants, so both they and the adult butterflies become toxic to predators and will make them ill if eaten.

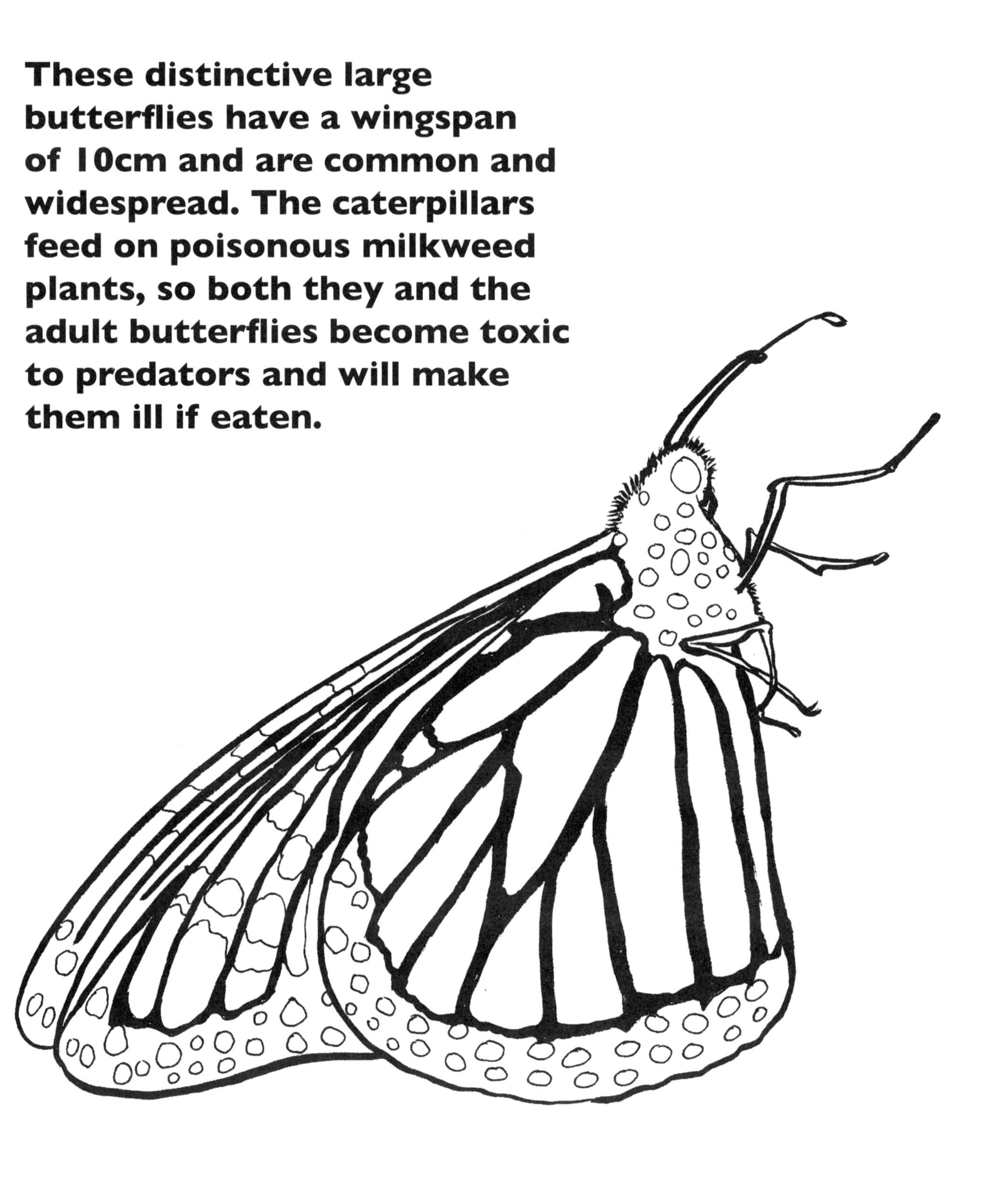

Wanderer Butterfly

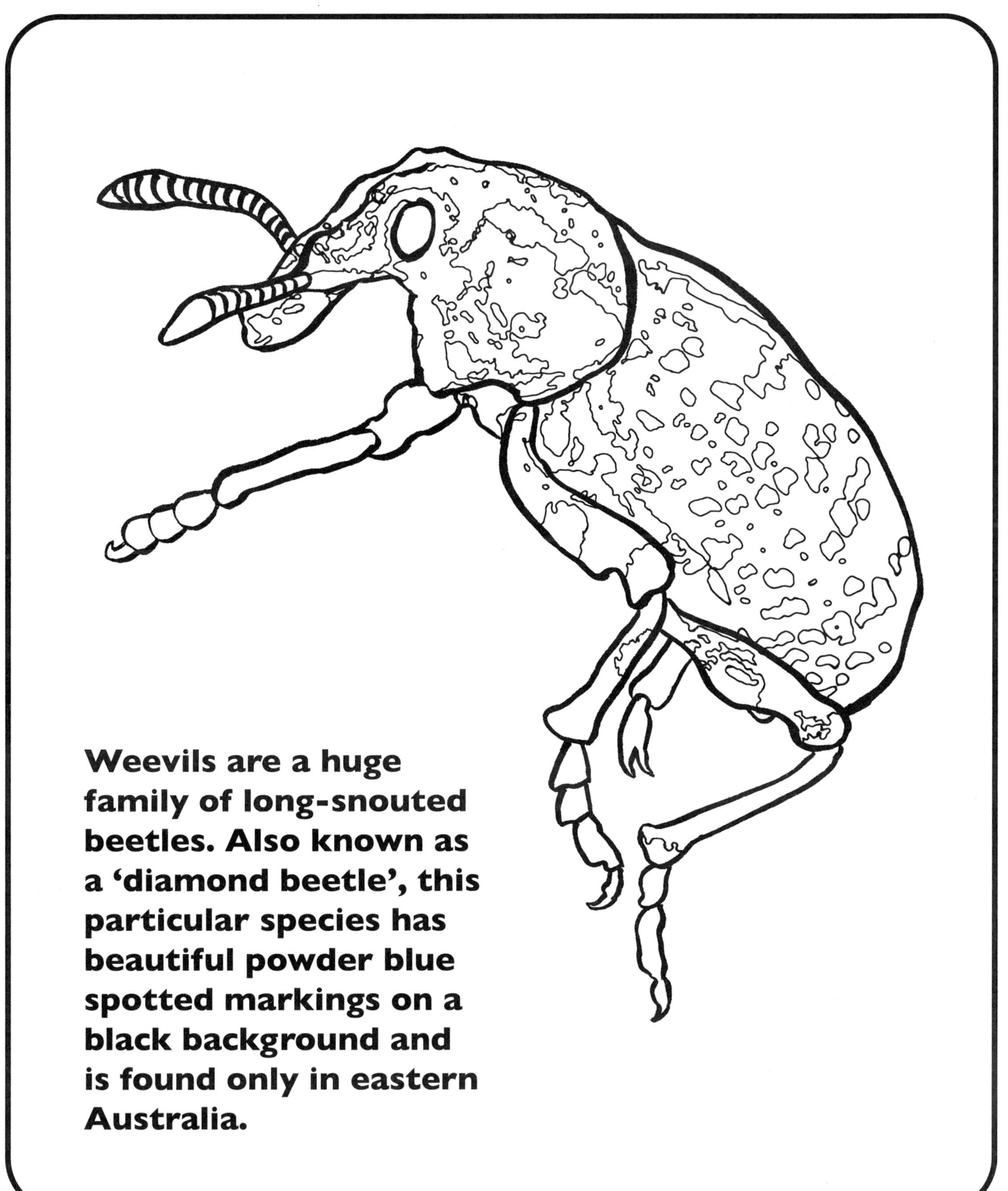

Weevils are a huge family of long-snouted beetles. Also known as a 'diamond beetle', this particular species has beautiful powder blue spotted markings on a black background and is found only in eastern Australia.

Botany Bay Weevil

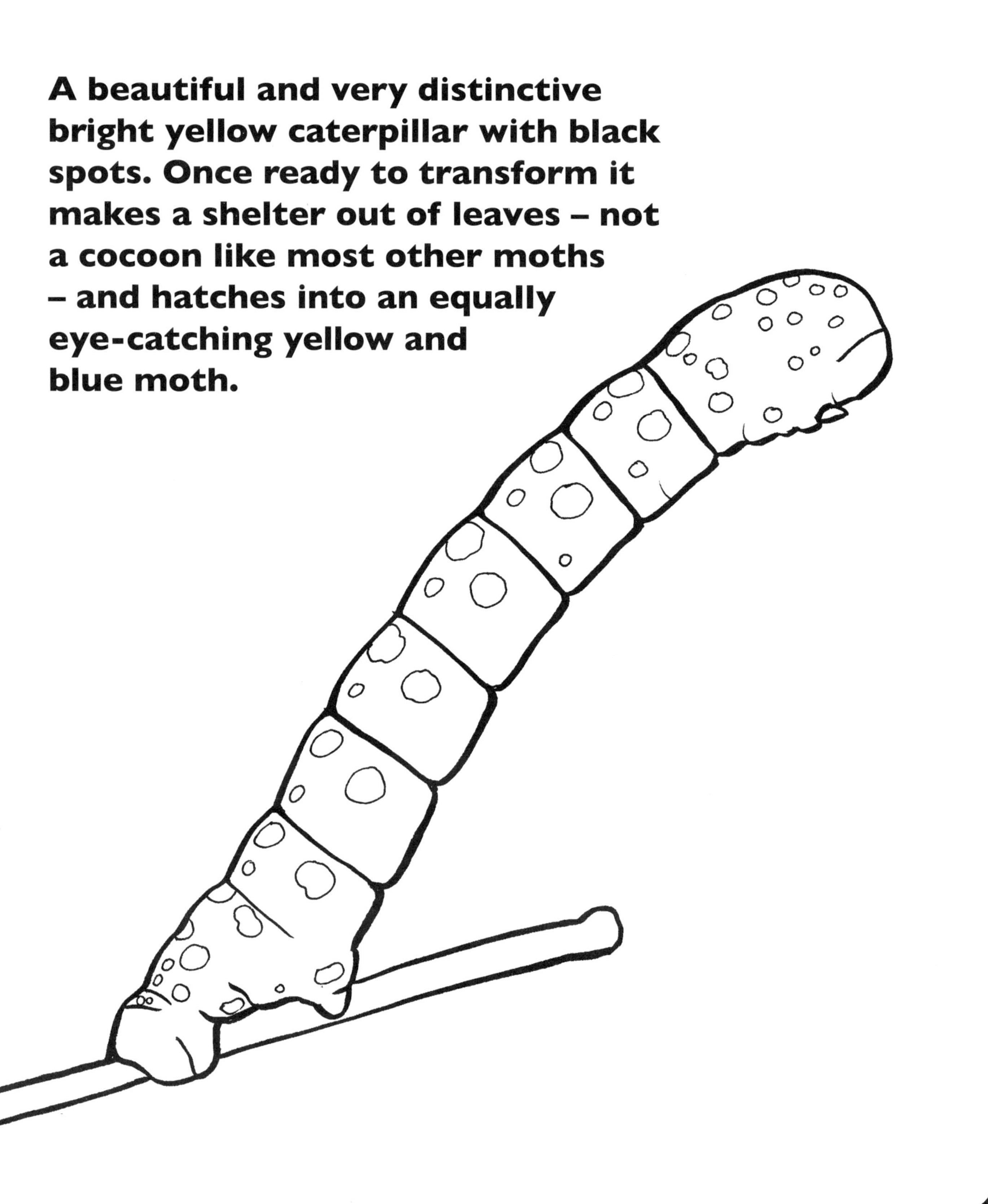

Four O'Clock Moth Caterpillar

These amazing insects or also known as praying mantises because their long front legs look like they are praying in a church. Voracious predators, they use these long forelegs to catch other insects to eat.

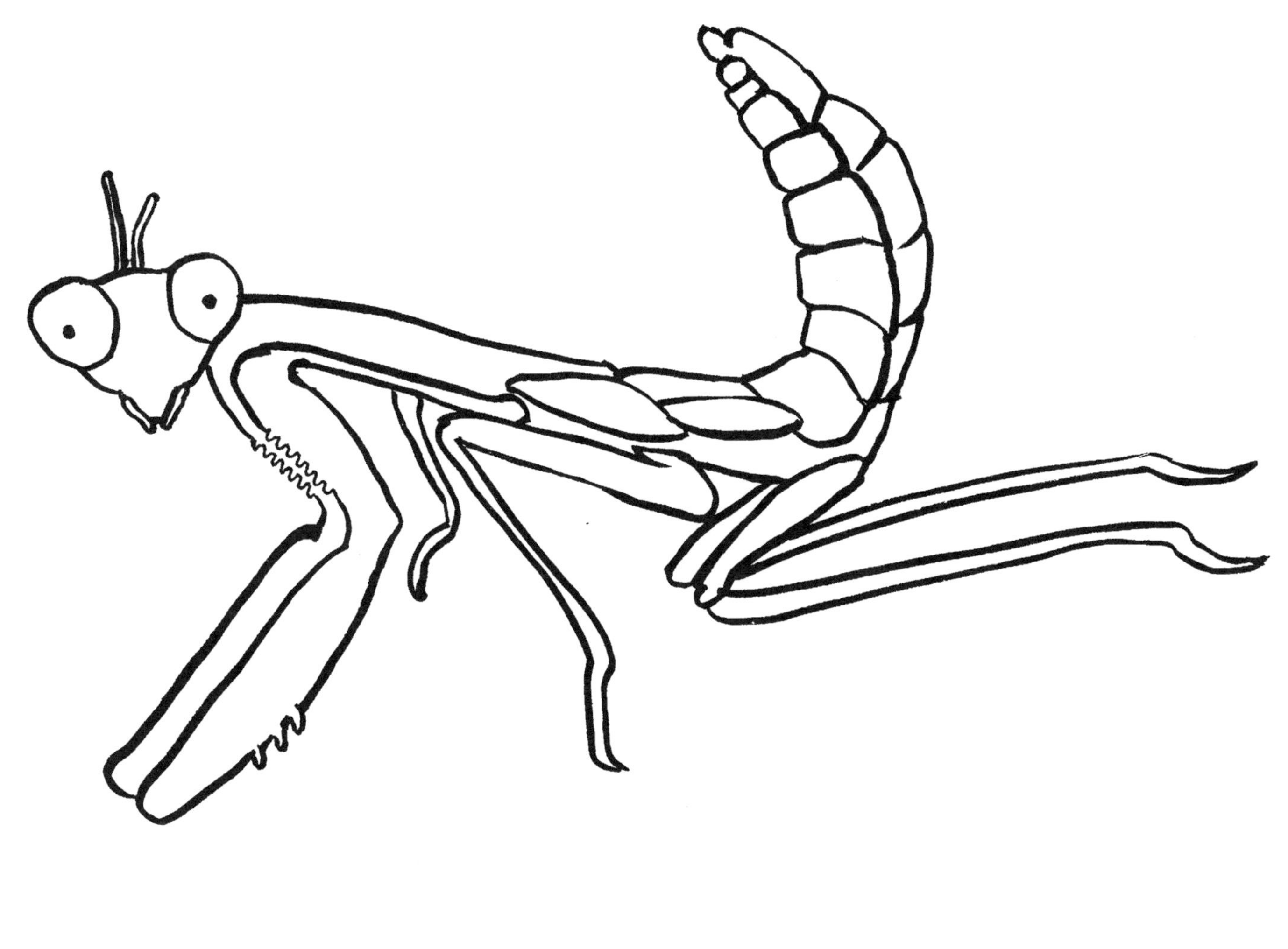

Mantid

Growing up to 4cm long, these big ants will vigorously defend themselves from danger and are known for their extremely painful sting. There are nearly 100 different species found all across Australia in a variety of habitats, from towns to forests.

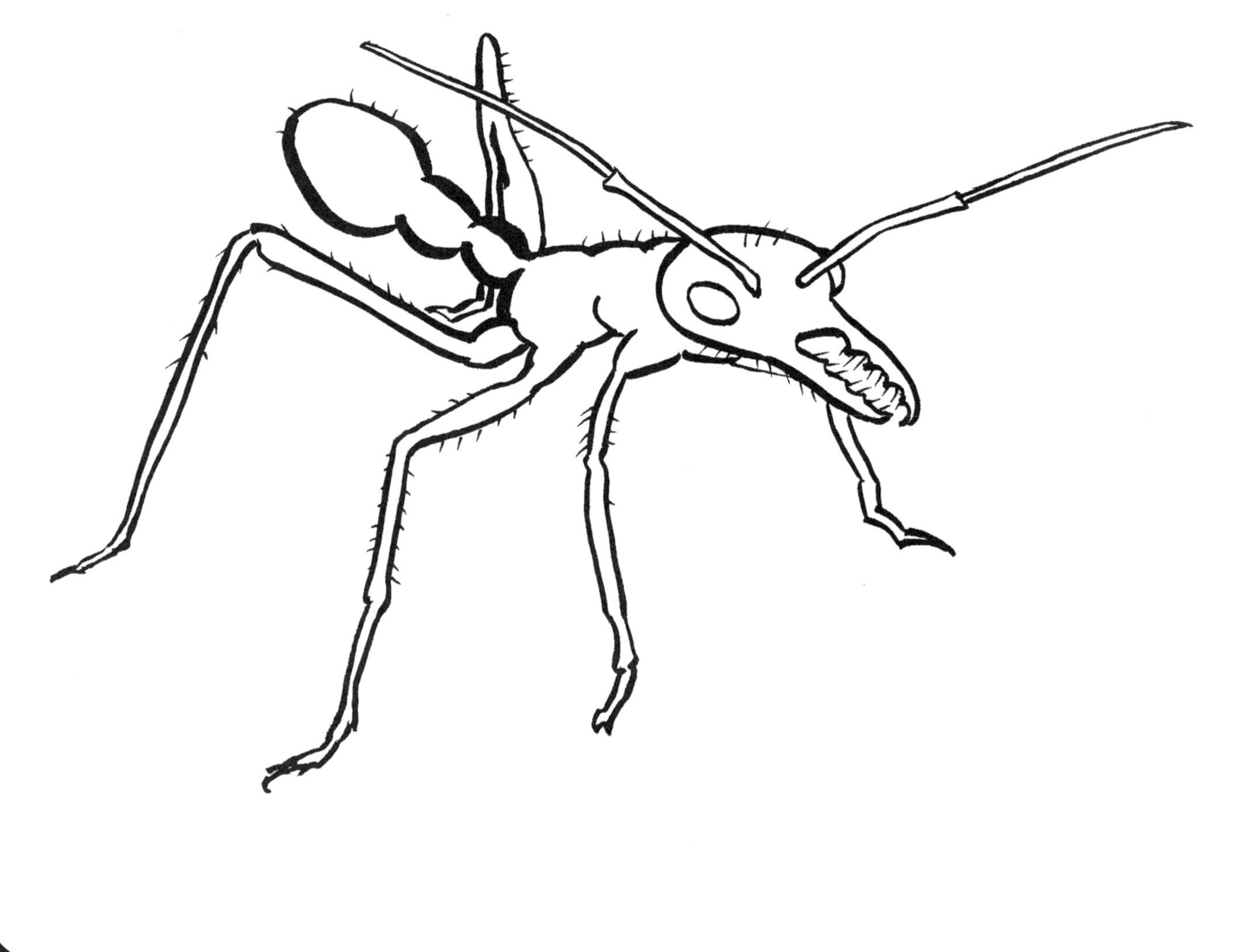

Bull Ant

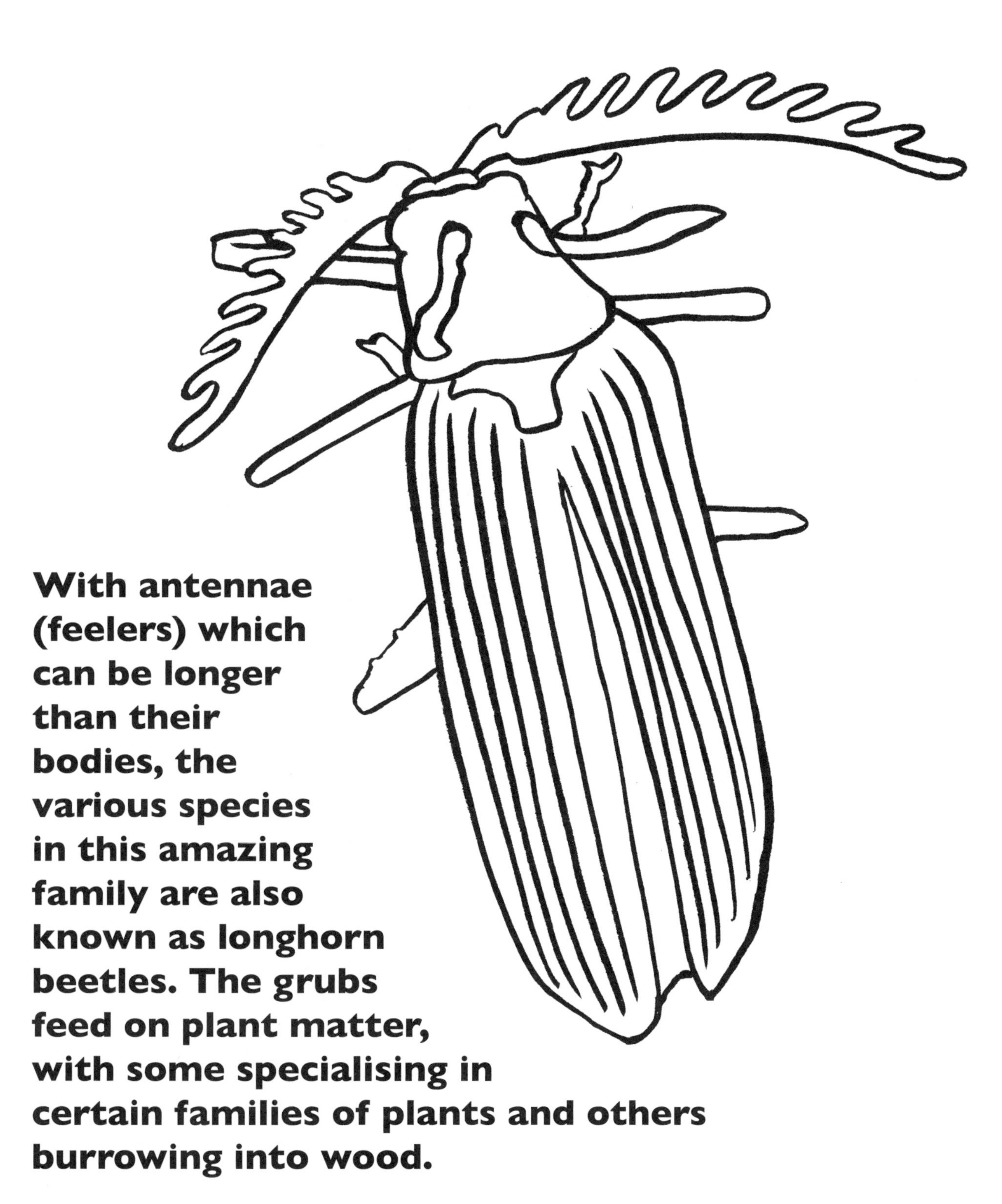

With antennae (feelers) which can be longer than their bodies, the various species in this amazing family are also known as longhorn beetles. The grubs feed on plant matter, with some specialising in certain families of plants and others burrowing into wood.

Longicorn Beetle

Nocturnal feeders on nectar, these beautiful large moths have a strong flight. They produce huge caterpillars that feed on a variety of plant species, including grapevines. There are many different species of hawkmoths in Australia.

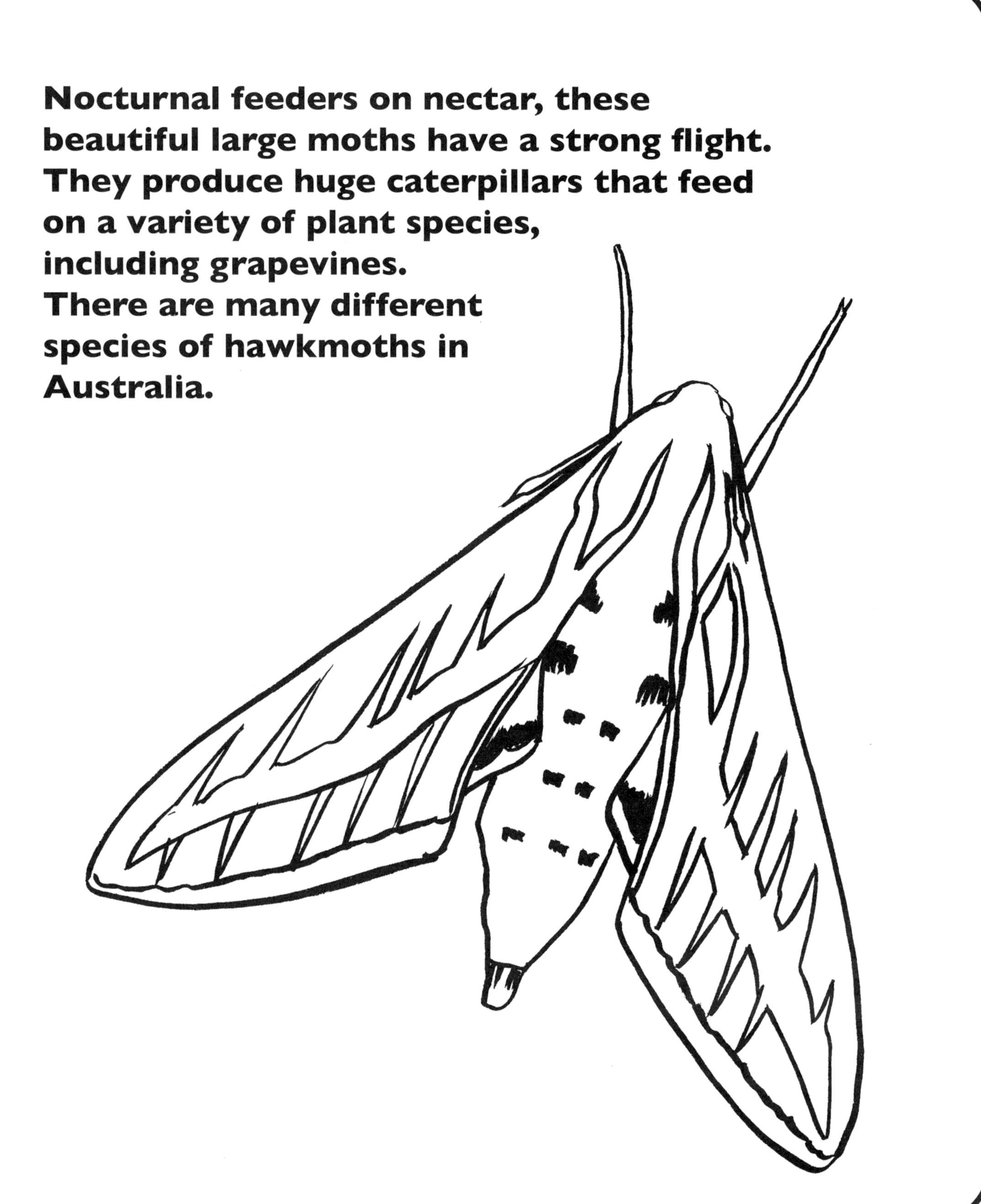

Vine Hawkmoth

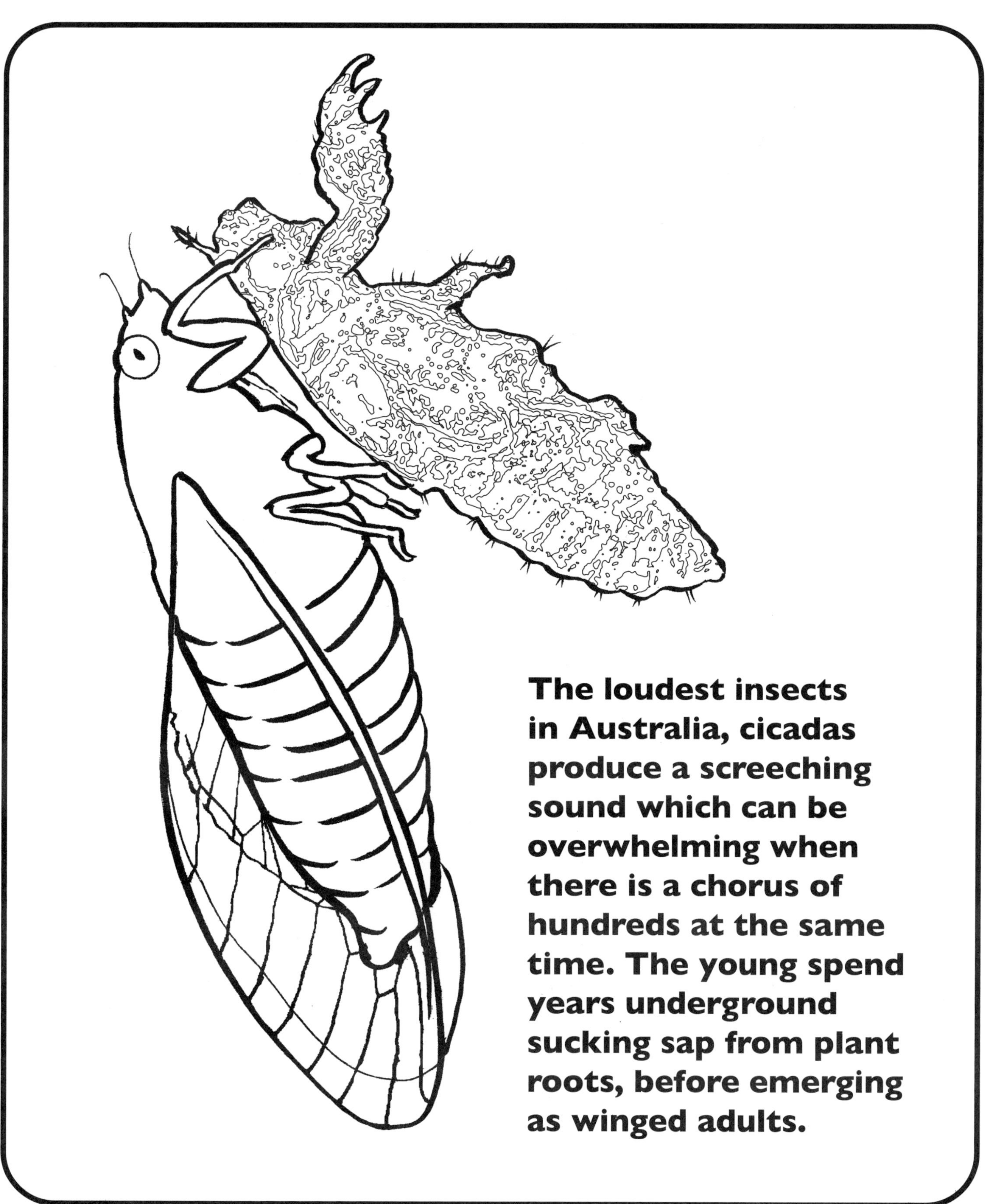

The loudest insects in Australia, cicadas produce a screeching sound which can be overwhelming when there is a chorus of hundreds at the same time. The young spend years underground sucking sap from plant roots, before emerging as winged adults.

Cicada

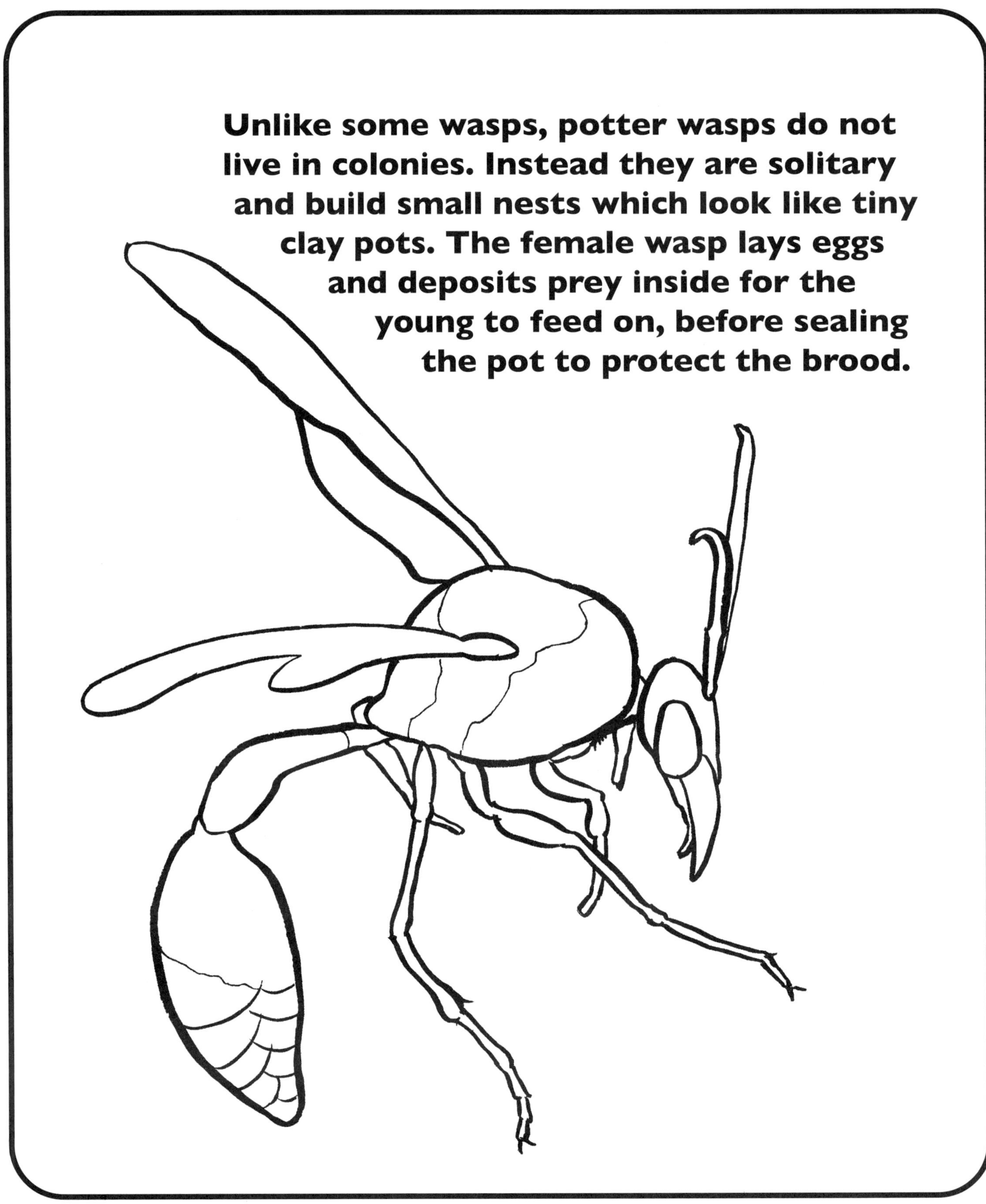
Unlike some wasps, potter wasps do not
live in colonies. Instead they are solitary
and build small nests which look like tiny
clay pots. The female wasp lays eggs
and deposits prey inside for the
young to feed on, before sealing
the pot to protect the brood.

Potter Wasp

Like a smaller version of a dragonfly, damselflies are part of the same family and can often be distinguished by their habit of folding their wings together behind their back. They are frequently found near water and catch insect prey in flight. There are many different species in various colours.

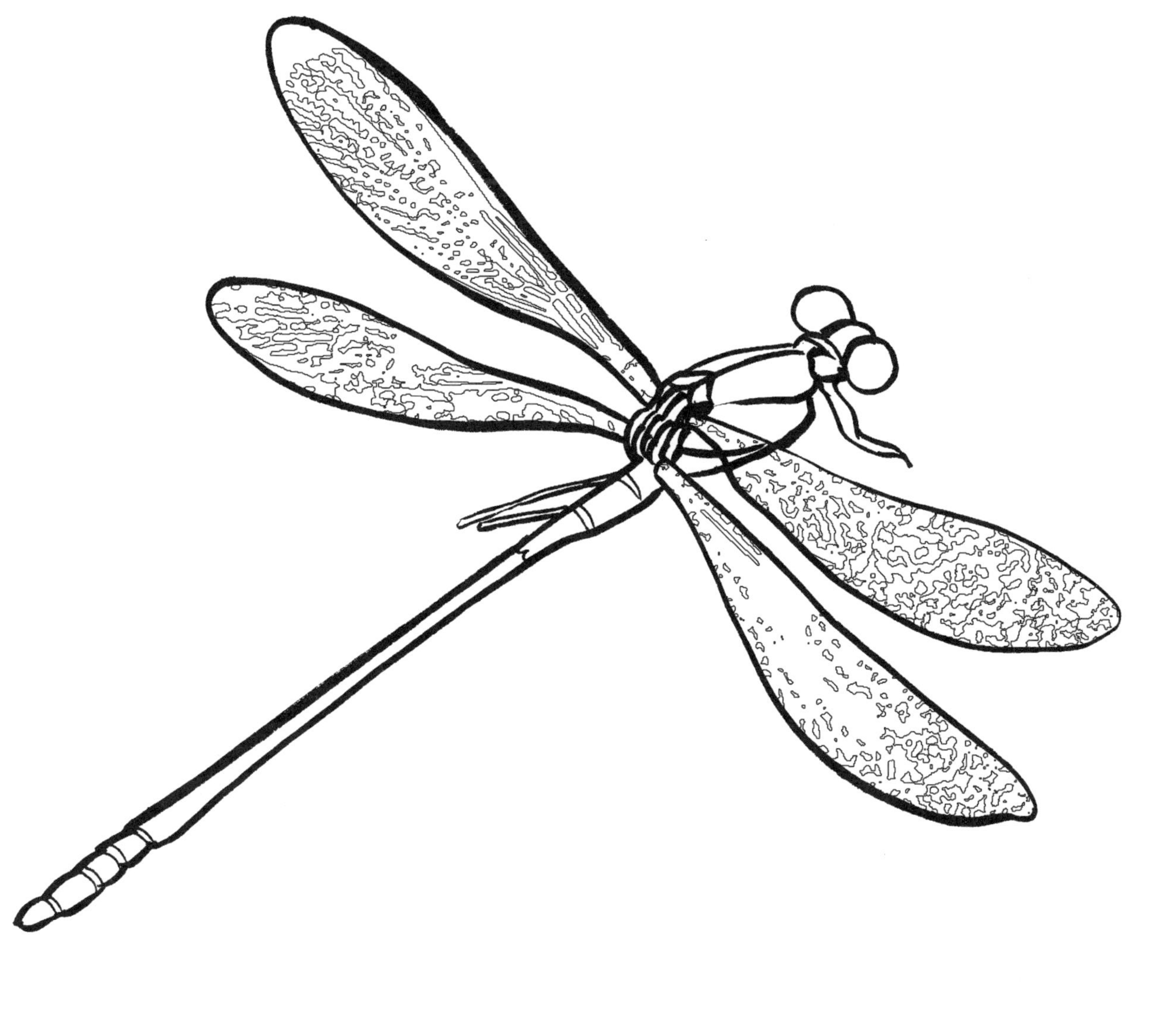

Damselfly

Published in 2023 by Reed New Holland Publishers
Sydney • Auckland

Level 1, 178 Fox Valley Road, Wahroonga, NSW 2076, Australia

newhollandpublishers.com

A record of this book is held at the National Library of Australia.

ISBN 978 1 92158 062 8

Managing Director: Fiona Schultz
Publisher and Project Editor: Simon Papps
Designer and illustrator: Andrew Davies
Production Director: Arlene Gippert
Printed in China

10 9 8 7 6 5 4 3 2 1

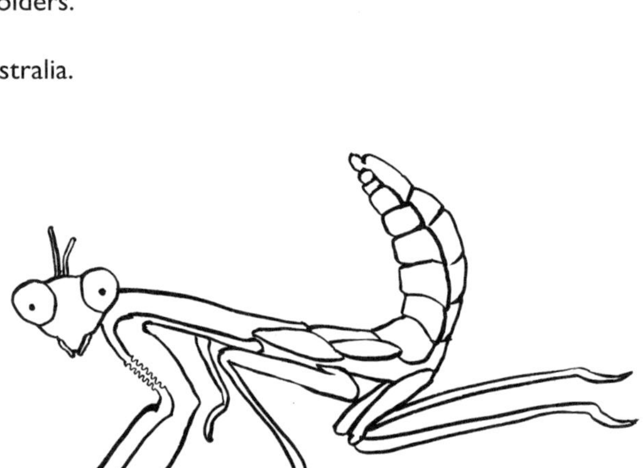

Also available from Reed New Holland:

Australian Birds: Colour and Learn
ISBN 978 1 76079 426 2
Australian Animals: Colour and Learn
ISBN 978 1 76079 432 3
Australian Butterflies: Colour and Learn
ISBN 978 1 76079 465 1
Australian Reptiles: Colour and Learn
ISBN 978 1 76079 464 4
Australian Fishes: Colour and Learn
ISBN 978 1 92158 063 5
Colour With Chris Humfrey's Awesome Australian Animals
ISBN 978 1 76079 424 8
Chris Humfrey's Awesome Australian Animals
ISBN 978 1 92554 670 5
Chris Humfrey's Coolest Creepy Crawlies
ISBN 978 1 76079 445 3

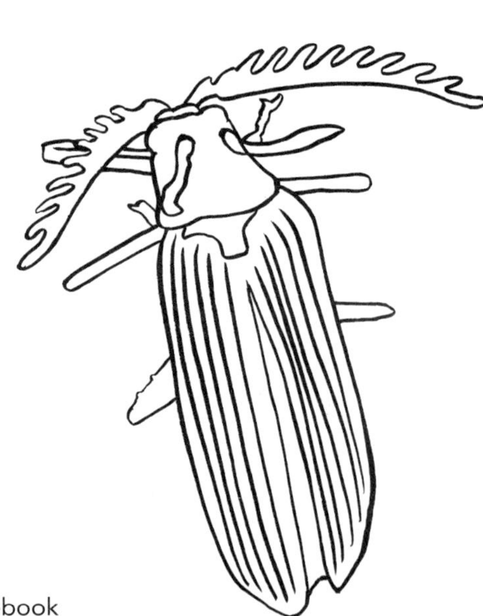

For details of hundreds of other Natural History titles see newhollandpublishers.com

And keep up with Reed New Holland and New Holland Publishers on Facebook

ReedNewHolland and NewHollandPublishers

@newhollandpublishers